Created by Pendleton Ward

Written by Danielle Corsetto

Illustrated by Zack Sterling

Additional Pencils by JJ Harrison

Inks by Stephanie Hocutt

Tones by Amanda Lafrenais

Letters by Mad Rupert

"Adventure Time with BMO!" by Meredith McClaren

Tones by Amanda Lafrenais

Cover by Stephanie Gonzaga

Colors by Kassandra Heller

Assistant Editor: Whitney Leopard

Editor: Shannon Watters

Designer: Stephanie Gonzaga

With Special Thanks to Marisa Marionakis, Rick Blanco, Curtis Lelash, Laurie Halal-Ono,
Keith Mack, Kelly Crews and the wonderful folks at Cartoon Network.

PLAYING WITH FIRE

ADVENTURE TIME Playing With Fire
ISBN: 978-1-78276-025-2

Published by Titan Comics, a division of Titan Publishing Group Ltd., 144 Southwark St., London, SE1 0UP. ADVENTURE TIME, CARTOON NETWORK, the logos, and all related characters and elements are trademarks of and © Cartoon Network. (S13) All rights reserved. All characters, events and institutions depicted herein are fictional. Any similarity between any of the names, characters, persons, events and/or institutions in this publication and actual names, characters and persons, whether living or dead, and/or institutions are unintended and purely coincidental.

A CIP catalogue record for this title is available from the British Library.

Printed in China.

First published in the USA and Canada in June 2013 by Kaboom! an imprint of BOOM! Studios.

10 9 8 7 6 5 4 3 2

We love to hear from our readers. Please email us at: **readercomments@titanemail.com**, or write to us at the above address.
For all the latest news, information, competitions and exclusive offers, sign up to our latest newsletter at:
www.titan-comics.com

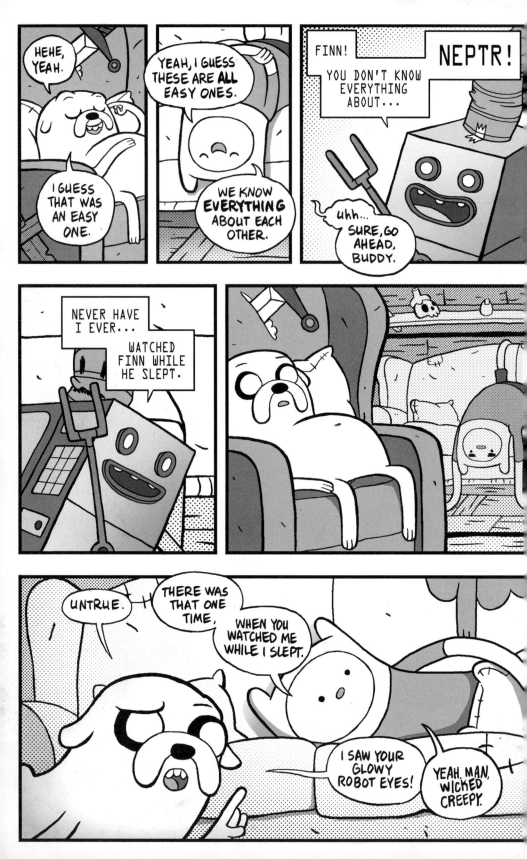

THERE IT IS...

THE SWORD AND THE SLURF GAME!

PICK A PRIZE, PRINCESS.

OOOOHH!

AAAHHH!

Y'LIKE THE NECKY ONE, YAH?

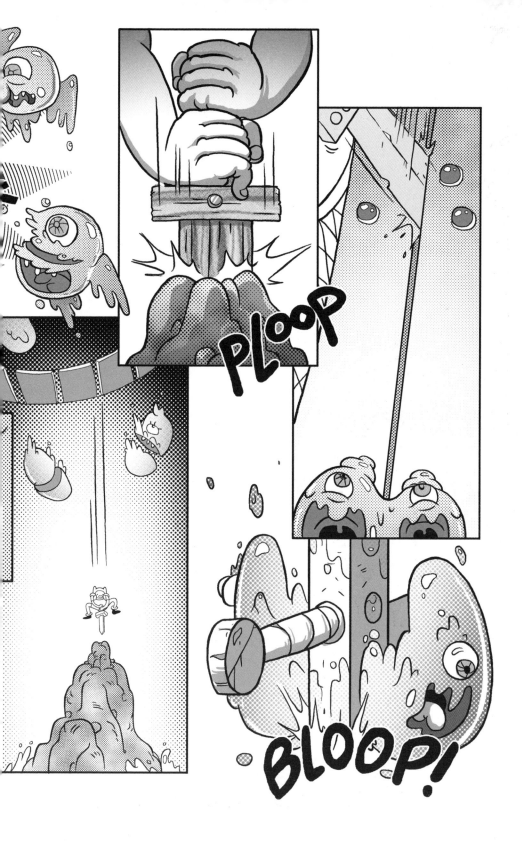

PLOOP

BLOOP!

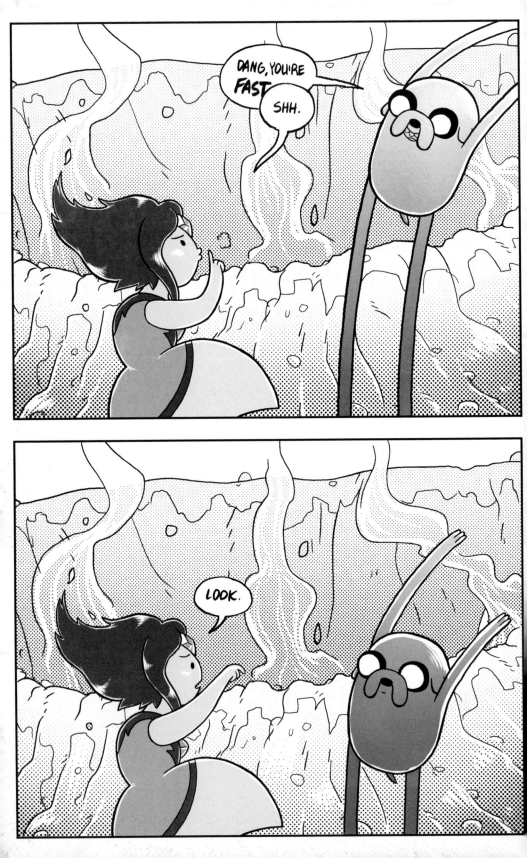

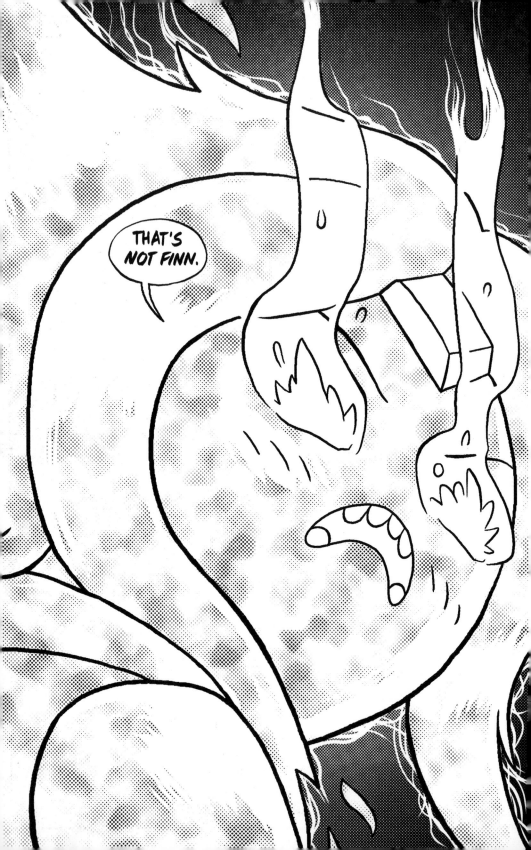

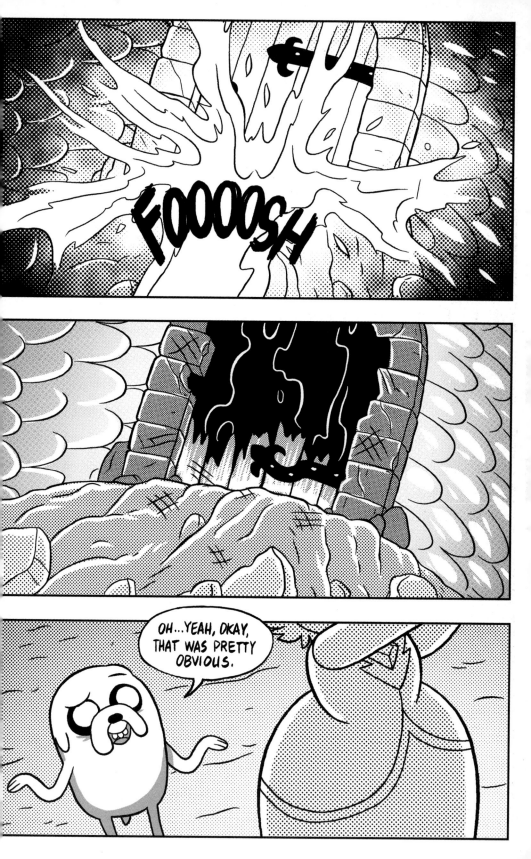

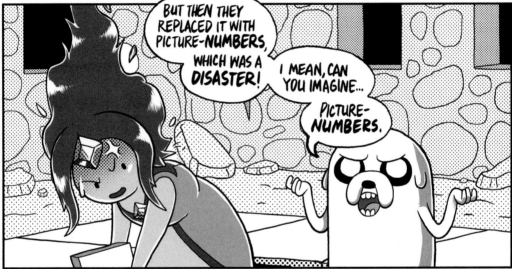

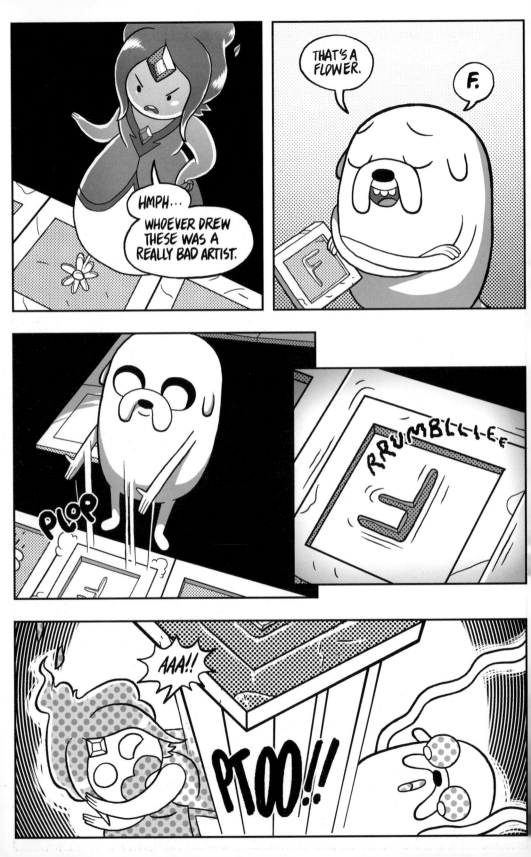

FOOSH!

AAAAAAA!!

FOOO—

TSSsss

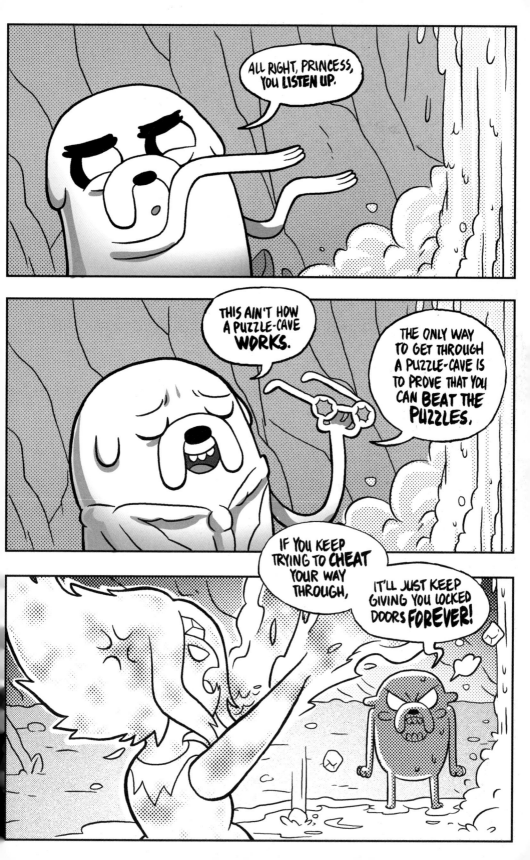

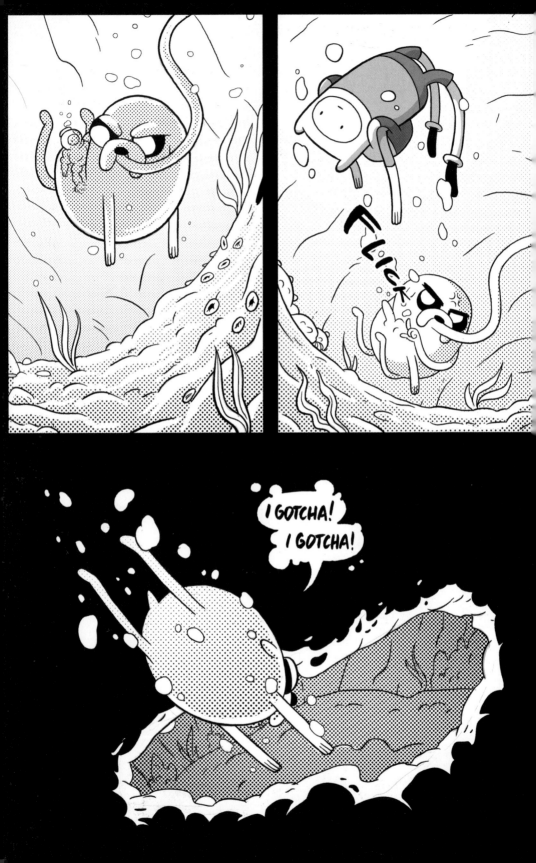

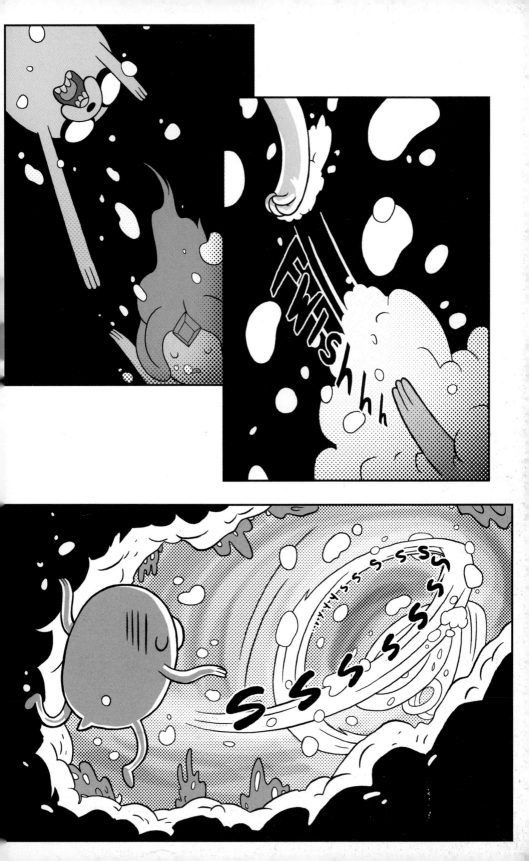

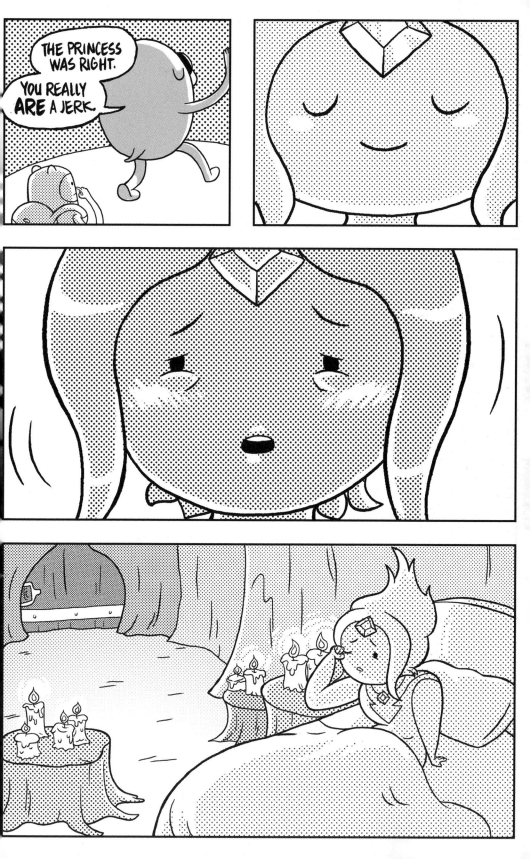

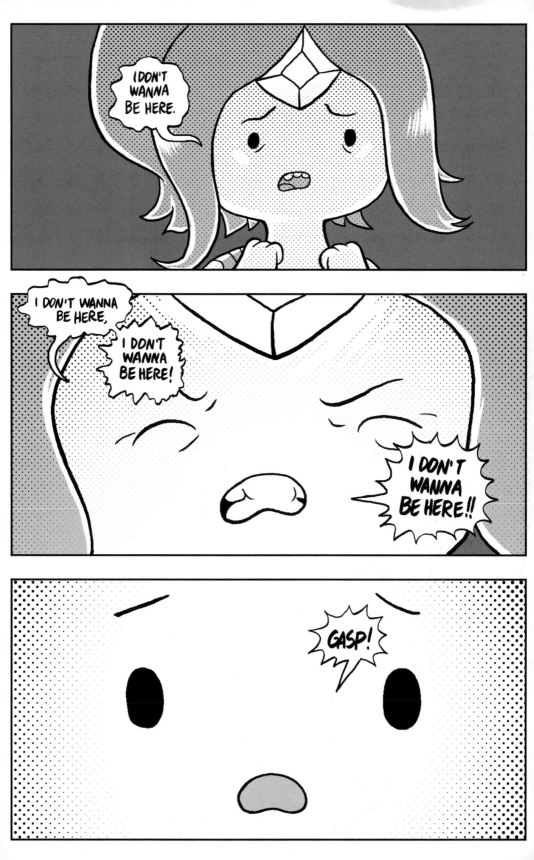

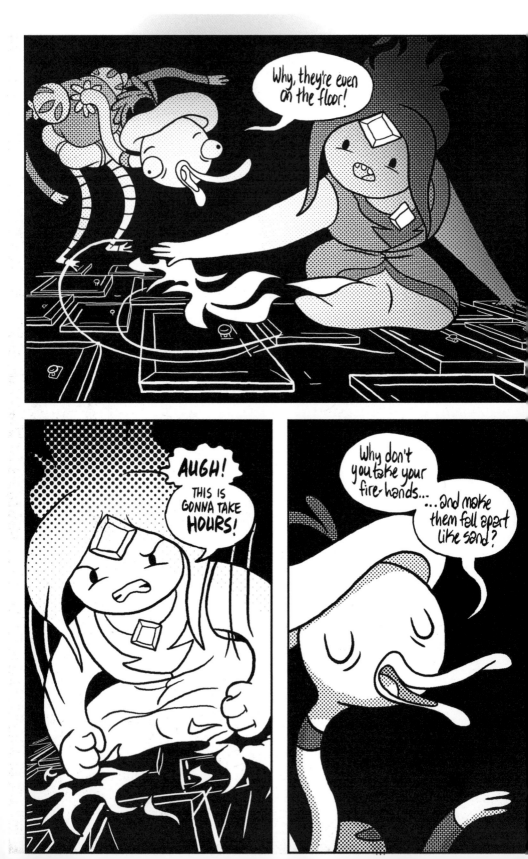

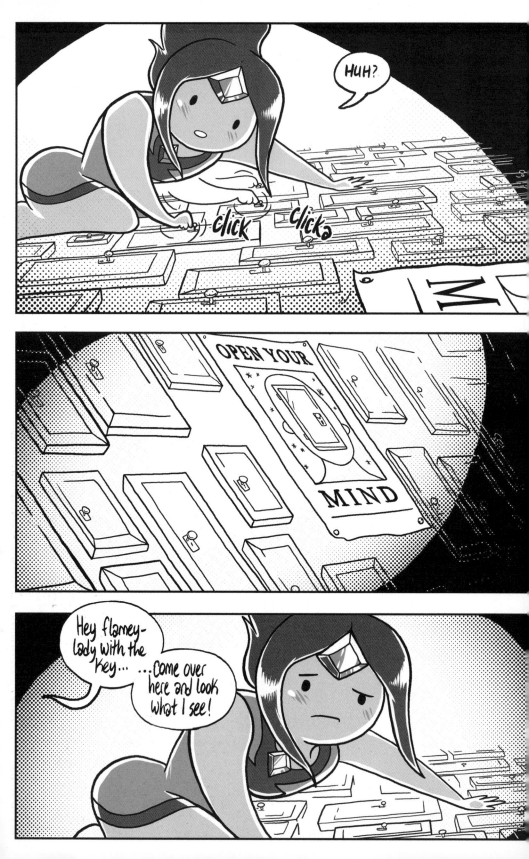

FSSSSSSSSSSHHHHH

FUH— FLAME PRINCESS?

Oh, that was all I needed.
That was REAL.
Bravo!
WHAT WAS THAT, SOME KIND OF SET-UP?
NO!
no no no no no!
Well... yes.
I mean.
Yeah, okay.
Yeah.
You see...
I have never known LOVE until now.

THE END

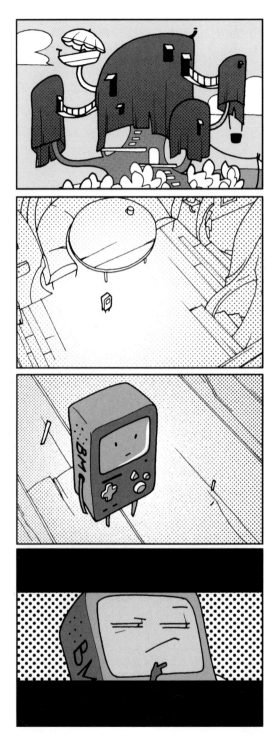

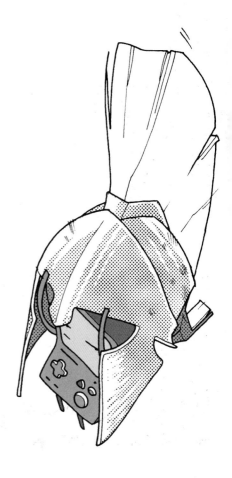

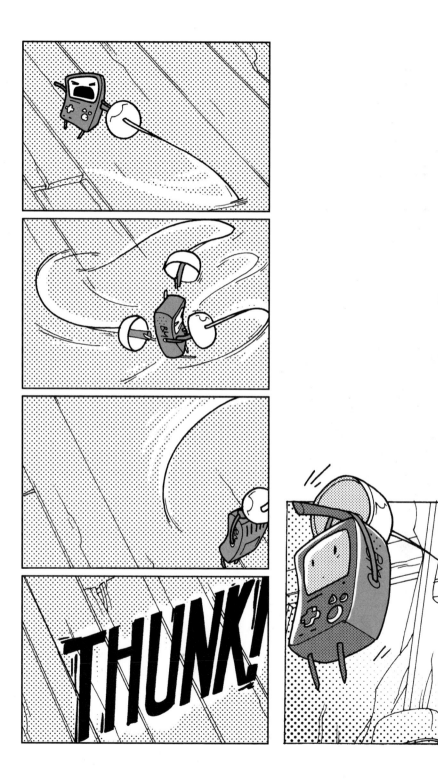

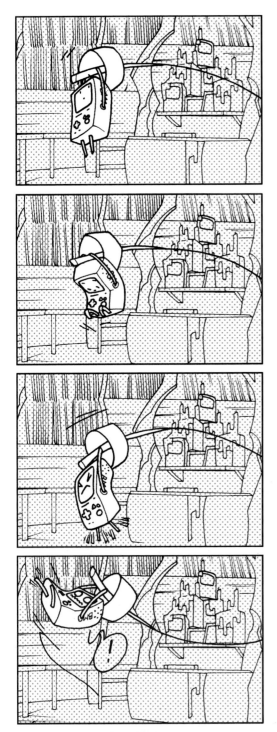

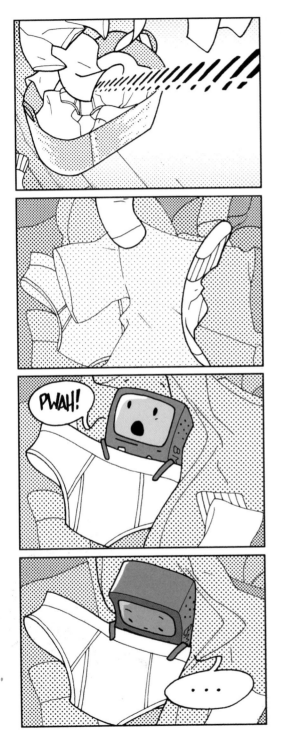

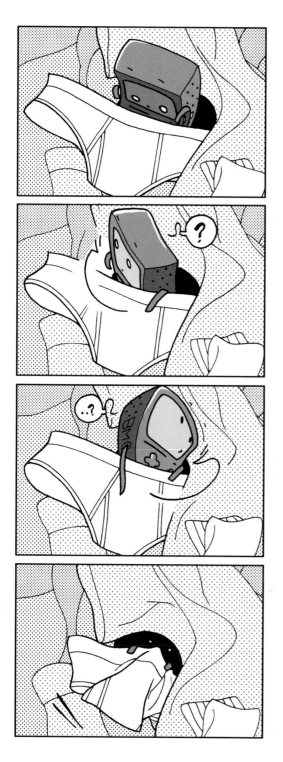

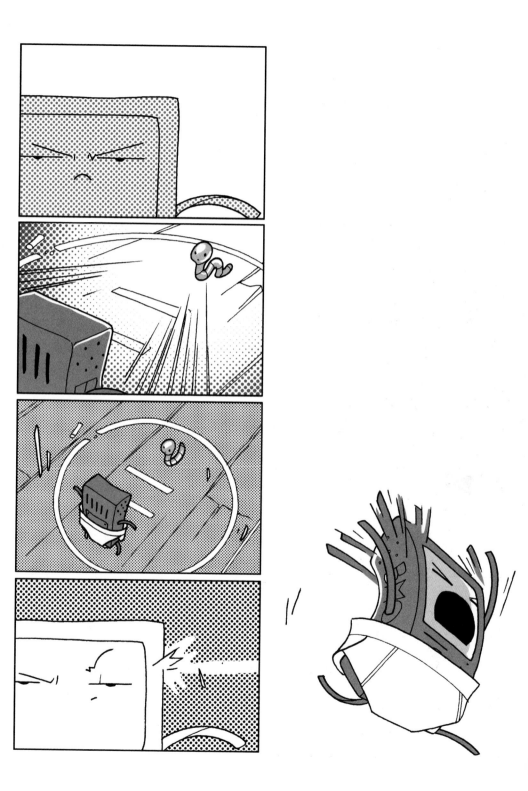

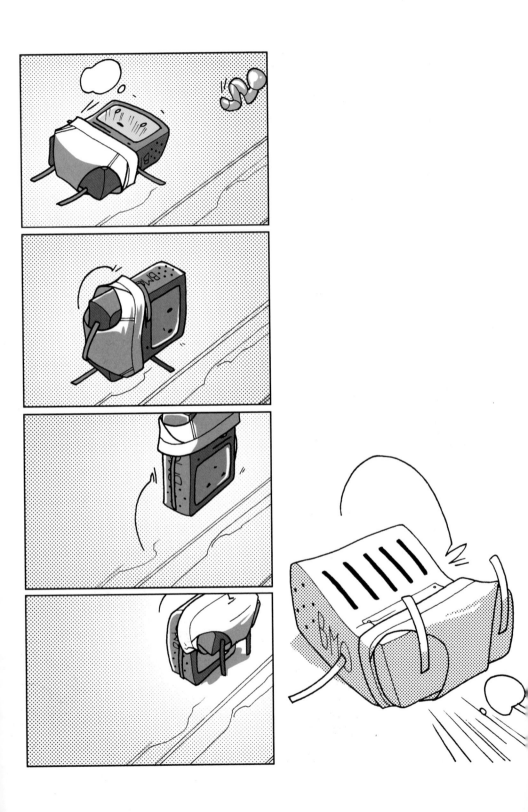

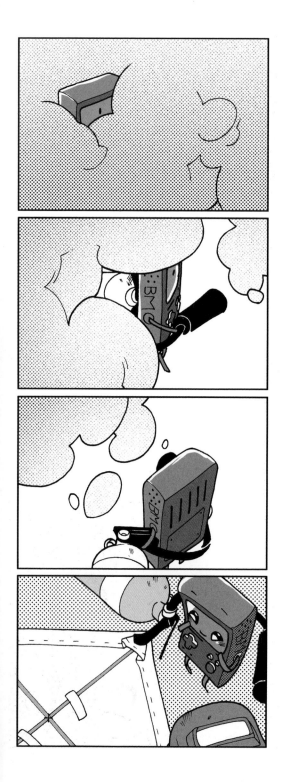

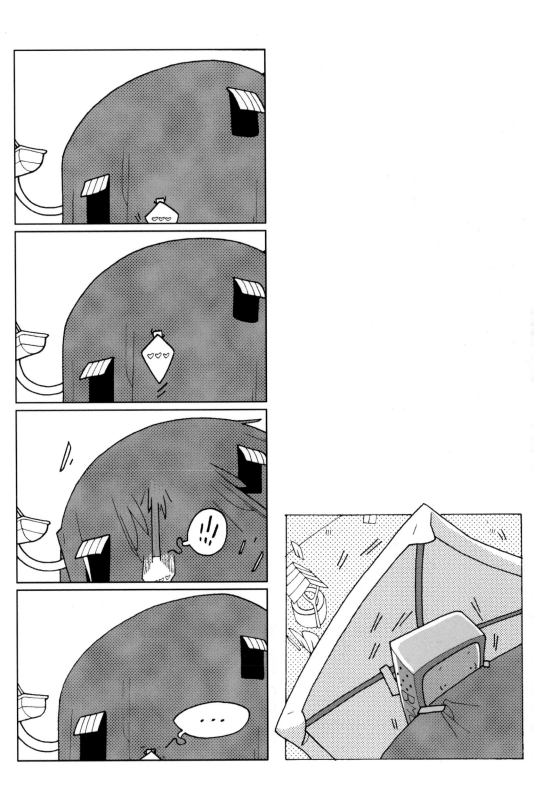

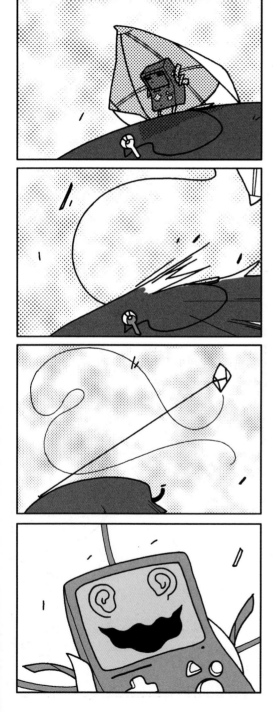

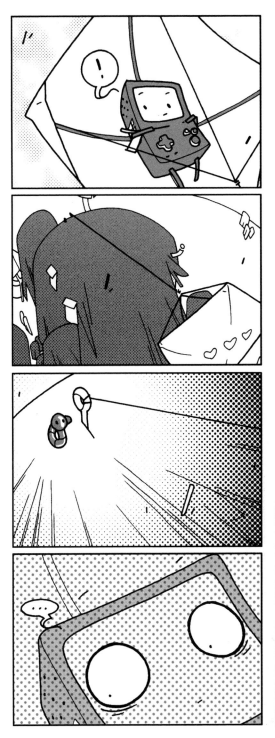

Volume 2
September 2013

Written by Danielle Corsetto & Illustrated by Zack Sterling